Pete the Cat

Saves Christmas

Pete the Cat

Saves Christmas

Written by
Eric Litwin

Art by
James Dean
(creator of Pete the Cat)

SCHOLASTIC INC.

ISBN 978-0-545-64913-1

Copyright © by James Dean (for the character of Pete the Cat).
Copyright © 2012 by James Dean and Eric Litwin.
All rights reserved. Published by Scholastic Inc., 557 Broadway, New York, NY 10012,
by arrangement with HarperCollins Children's Books, a division of HarperCollins Publishers.
SCHOLASTIC and associated logos are trademarks and/or registered
trademarks of Scholastic Inc.

12 11 10 9 8 7 6 5   14 15 16 17 18/0

Printed in the U.S.A.   40

First Scholastic printing, November 2013

The artist used pen and ink, with watercolor and acrylic paint on
300lb hot press paper to create the illustrations for this book.
Typography by Jeanne L. Hogle

'Twas the day before Christmas and Santa was ill.
In the cold winter wind he had caught a bad chill.

Will Christmas be canceled?
Will it come to that?
"Never!"
cried Santa. "Let's call
Pete the Cat!"

Santa asked Pete
to deliver the toys
to all the good girls
and to all the good boys.

"I'll do it!" said Pete.

"And although I am small,
at Christmas we give,
so I'll give it my all."

Pete jumped in his minibus and started to roll.

"Road trip!" cried Pete.

"First stop—the North Pole."

The reindeer were waiting to give Pete a tow,

so he packed up the presents and told them to go.

Then the minibus flew, just like in a movie.

Pete the Cat cried, "This is totally

groovy!"

Give it your all, give it your all.
At Christmas we give,
so give it your all.

As the children were sleeping all snug in their beds,

Pete and his reindeer appeared overhead.

Straight down the chimney Pete flew in a dash,
then back in his minibus quick as a flash.

Each time he delivered a holiday gift,
he crossed off a name written on Santa's list.

Santa's list was so big, and Pete felt so small.
But at Christmas we give, so he gave it his all.

♫

Give it your all, give it your all.
At Christmas we give,
so give it your all.

♫

MICHAEL
JACOB
MADISON
MATTHEW
PIPER
EMILY
SAVANNAH
SOPHIA
ERIC
EMMA
OLIVIA
JESSICA
TREY
DESTINY
JOSH
HELEN
DORSEY
KIM
JAMES
JACKIE
JOHN
JANET
SARAH
GRACE
DAVID

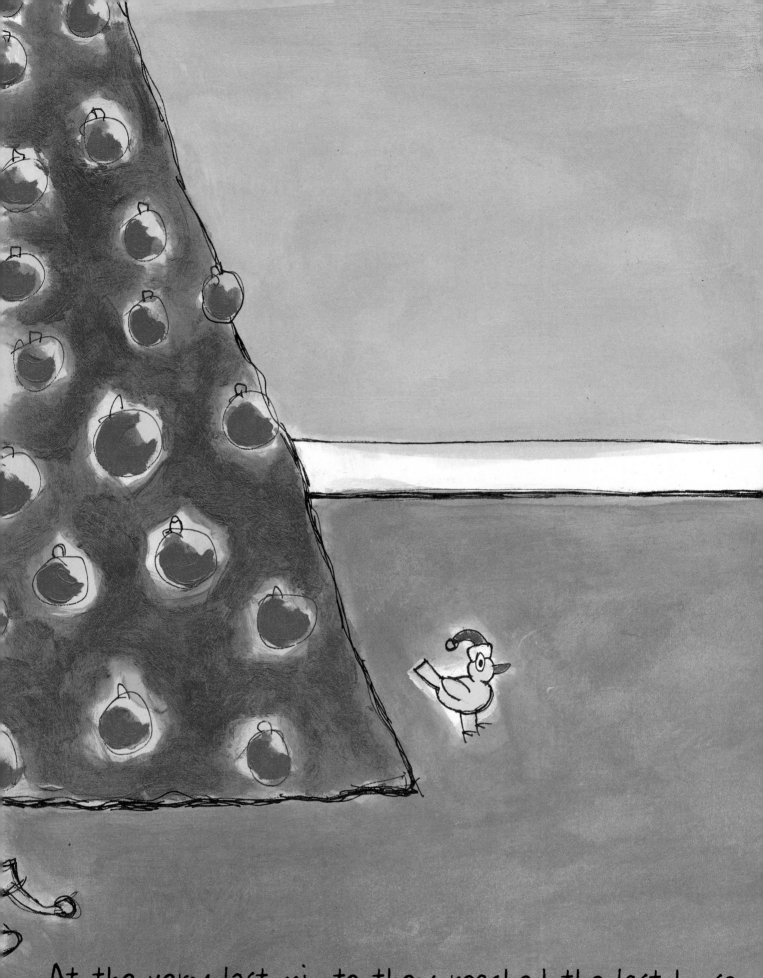

At the very last minute they reached the last house.

Pete dashed in and out just as quiet as a mouse.

Then right at the break of the new Christmas Day,

Pete and his reindeer were flying away.

Back at the North Pole, old Santa was waiting.
The elves and the townsfolk were all celebrating.

Santa was dressed in his red coat and hat and cried,

"Hip hip hurray for our

Friend Pete the Cat."